THIS BOOK BELONGS TO

_ _

COWHIDE-AND-SEEK

by SHERI DILLARD
Illustrated by JESS PAUWELS

RP | KIDS
PHILADELPHIA

Thank you to my wonderful editors, Julie Matysik and Adrienne Szpyrka,
the RPK team, dedicated agents Liza Fleissig and Ginger Harris-Dontzin, my talented
and inspiring critique groups, Crumpled Paper and Critcasters, and finally, to Mom,
Dad, and Debbie, who made my childhood a living picture book.

Running Press Kids
Hachette Book Group
1290 Avenue of the Americas, New York, NY 10104
www.runningpress.com/rpkids
@RP_Kids

Printed in China

First Edition: May 2019

Published by Running Press Kids, an imprint of Perseus Books, LLC, a subsidiary of Hachette Book
Group, Inc. The Running Press Kids name and logo is a trademark of the Hachette Book Group.

The Hachette Speakers Bureau provides a wide range of authors for speaking events.
To find out more, go to www.hachettespeakersbureau.com or call (866) 376-6591.

The publisher is not responsible for websites (or their content)
that are not owned by the publisher.

Print book cover and interior design by Frances J. Soo Ping Chow.

Library of Congress Control Number: 2018935978

ISBNs: 978-0-7624-9184-1 (hardcover), 978-0-7624-9185-8 (ebook),
978-0-7624-6634-4 (ebook), 978-0-7624-6633-7 (ebook)

APS

10 9 8 7 6 5 4 3 2 1

To my family, Bessie's first fans—Mark,
Michael, Cory, and Jacob
-S.D.

To our new life with our new friends
in the countryside
-J.P.

It was a typical day on the dairy farm.
But when Farmer Ted began counting his cattle,
"One, two, three, four . . ."

Bessie thought he was starting
a game of . . .

. . . cowhide-and-seek!
Bessie stood very still.
She didn't utter a moo.

But her hiding spot moved.

So Bessie moooved, too.

" . . . ninety-eight, ninety-nine, one hundred.
Where's Bessie?" asked Farmer Ted.

Just then . . .

Bessie found a better hiding spot.

But someone spotted her.
"I see a cow!" said a little boy.

Shhh, thought Bessie. *The farmer might hear you.*
"Moo," she explained, but the boy didn't understand.

Uh, oh. Bessie needed another place to hide. She moooved on.

Through a sandbox.

Under the swings.

Down a path.

"Where's Bessie?"

And then . . .

Bessie found an even better hiding spot.

But someone spotted her.
Breeeeeeet!

Shhh. Bessie offered to share her hiding spot. "Moo?"
But no one knew how to hide.

"Bessie?"

Uh, oh. Bessie needed another place to hide. She moooved on.

Past the goalie.

Down the sideline.

Through the fans.

"Where's Bessie?"

But then . . .

Bessie found an even *better* hiding spot.
It was mooovelous!

But someone spotted her.
"I found Bessie!"

Uh, oh. Bessie needed another place to hide.
And quick! "Moo!"

"Ready or not, here they come!"

"Bessie? Come out, come out, wherever you are!" Farmer Ted called.

Bessie ran fast. Farmer Ted ran fast.

Bessie ran faster. Farmer Ted ran faster.

Bessie ran her fastest. Farmer Ted ran his fastest.

Then . . .
Bessie found the perfect hiding spot. *Shhh.*

Where's Bessie? Can *you* find her?